# Daisy and the Beastie

## Jane Simmons

ORCHARD BOOKS

For Freyja and Oscar
and their weird parents

Other titles by Jane Simmons

*Come On, Daisy!*
*Daisy and the Egg*
*Daisy Says Coo!*
*Daisy's Day Out*
*Daisy's Favourite Things*
*Go To Sleep, Daisy*
*Ebb's New Friend*
*Ebb and the Greedy Gulls*

ORCHARD BOOKS
96 Leonard Street, London EC2A 4XD
*Orchard Books Australia*
14 Mars Road, Lane Cove, NSW 2066
1 86039 795 6 (hardback)
First published in Great Britain in 2000
Copyright © Jane Simmons 2000
The right of Jane Simmons to be identified as the author and illustrator of this work has been
asserted by her in accordance with the Copyright, Designs and Patents Act, 1988.
A CIP catalogue record for this book is available from the British Library.
1 3 5 7 9 10 8 6 4 2
Printed in Singapore

Grandpa was just finishing Daisy's favourite story.
"...they searched the farm, but no one found
the Beastie!" he said.
"Coo," said Daisy.

Grandpa slowly closed his eyes and began to snore.
"Don't worry," said Daisy. "We'll find the Beastie!"
"Beastie," said Pip.

"The Beastie might be with the chickens,"
said Daisy.

"Cheep, cheep," chirped the chicks.

"Cheep," said Pip.

"...or hiding with the geese."
"Beep! beep!" said the goslings.
"Beep!" said Pip.

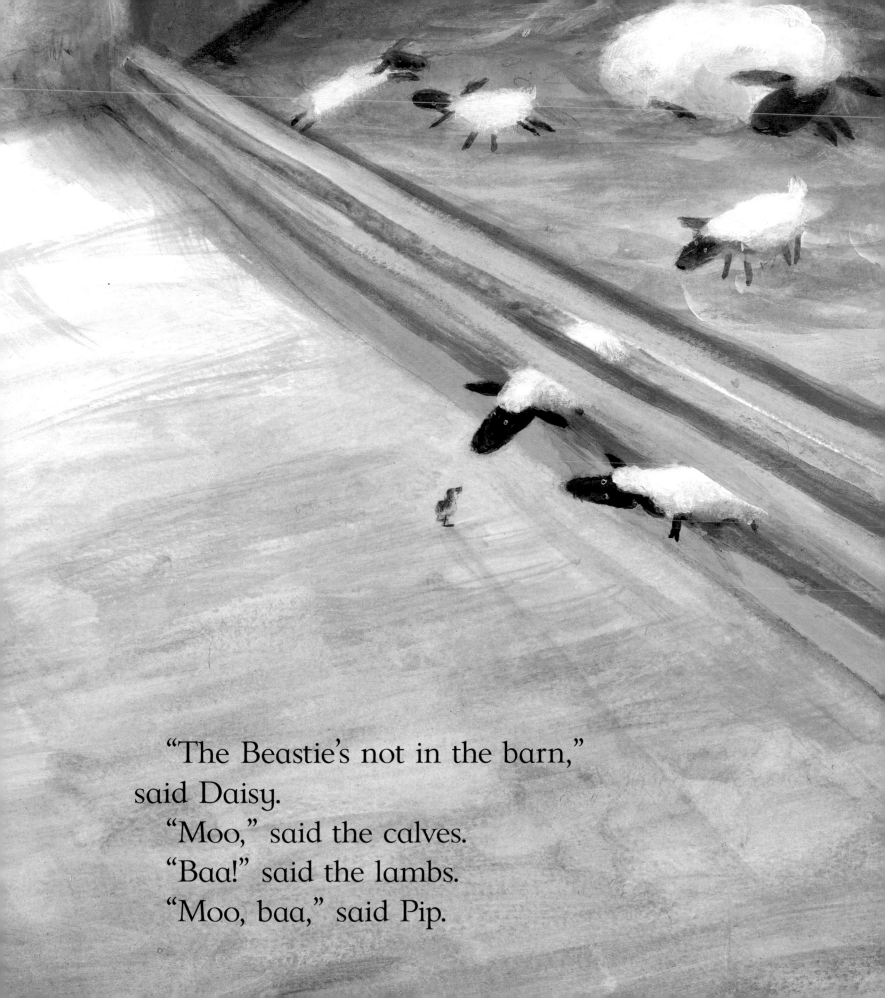

"The Beastie's not in the barn,"
said Daisy.
"Moo," said the calves.
"Baa!" said the lambs.
"Moo, baa," said Pip.

"...or in the meadow."
"Buzz," buzzed the bees.
"Buzz," said Pip.

There was no Beastie in the pig sty.
"Wee, wee," squealed the piglets.
"Wee," said Pip.

...nor in the orchard.
Hoppity hop, hop!
Just then...

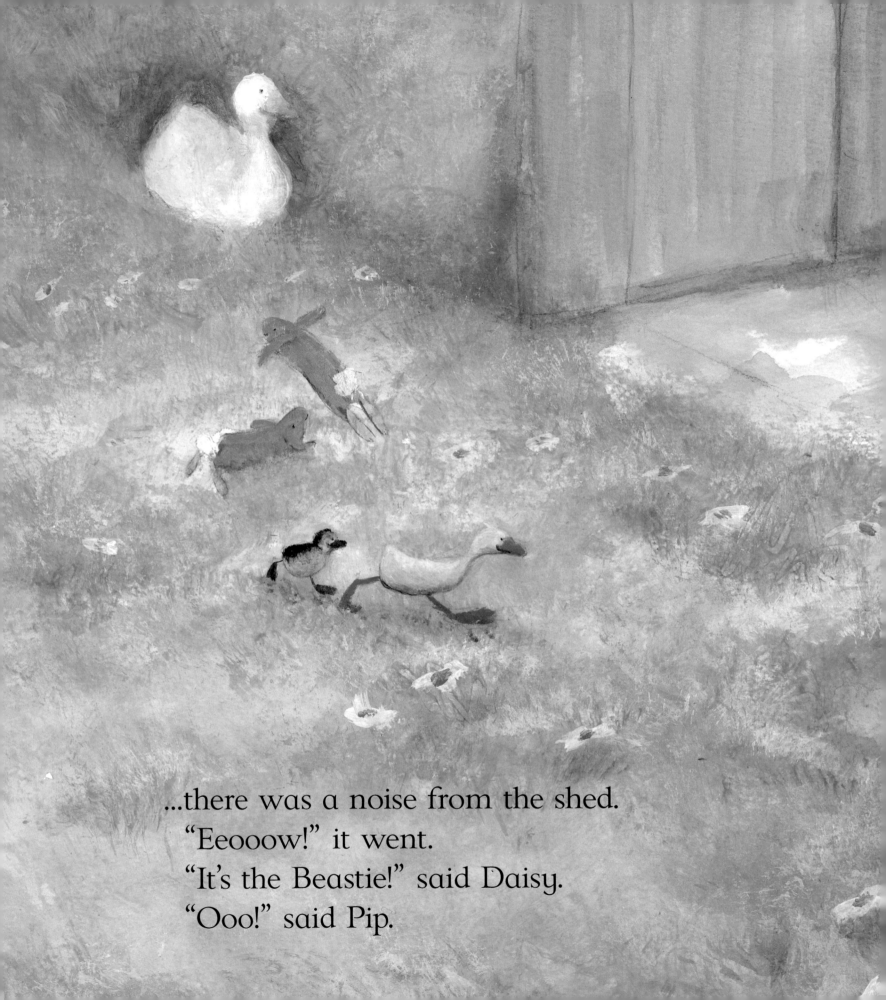

...there was a noise from the shed.
"Eeooow!" it went.
"It's the Beastie!" said Daisy.
"Ooo!" said Pip.

Daisy and Pip
couldn't see anything.

As they crept forward,
something rumbled,
"MEEEE..."

"It's the Beastie! Run, Pip, run!"
cried Daisy.

"We found the Beastie!"
"The Beastie!" said Grandpa. "Where?"
"THERE!"

"Meooow," said the kittens.
"Coo," said Daisy.
"Coo," said Pip.
Grandpa laughed...

...and Daisy and Pip played
with all the kitten beasties.